The Christmas Quilt

By

David M. Gullstrand

DEDICATED TO

My three wonderful grandchildren; Vada Grace, Clara Jo, and their new baby brother Baker Edward. These 3 kids a so lucky to have my Son Grant and his wife Jenny to be their daddy and mommy.

I love you all.

ACKNOWLEDGMENTS

I'd like to thank my Creative Writing teacher at ROVA High School for challenging my writing skills. Thank you Coach Renwick, I couldn't have done any of this without your guidance. I also need to thank my parents, Ed and Sandy for never giving up on me and pushing to accomplish whatever my goals might be.

CONTENTS

CHAPTER ONE
THE HOMECOMING

Good evening, this is Barbra Lancaster reporting with Channel 4 News. We are here in Faith, Vermont, awaiting the return of Sergeant First Class Sugar Smithhouse. I'm standing here with her husband, who is the Sheriff of High Point, West Virginia. By his side are Stella and Stanley, Sugar's two children.

We are at the Lawson Inn, which has been owned and operated by Sugar's parents and now her sister, Cookie, for the past two generations. Smithhouse has been in Afghanistan for the past 10 months, and the family is anxious and excited for her to get home in time for her sister's Easter wedding.

But the real story here is not the homecoming or the wedding—it's that Sugar finally gets to meet her Aunt Eve Olson Watson. Eve and her twin sister, Christmas Watson, were tragically separated 63 years ago. They were victims of the infamous 1960 fire that destroyed the Appleton Convent and Orphanage.

The orphanage and all of its records were a total loss, and tragically, 12 nuns perished in the fire. But first, they made sure that all of the children made it out alive. The aftermath was total chaos, and the 48 orphans, ranging in age from 8 to three months, were quickly placed wherever they could find a safe place. The night of the fire, the only identification the children had were their first names sewn on their pajamas.

Sadly, the twin sisters, Christmas and Eve, were too young to speak up for themselves. That night was the last time the twins ever saw each other. We are now blessed to be joined by Eve Olson Watson, a 66-year-old widow from Cumberland, Maine.

"Someone get Cookie to come over and join us," called out the reporter.

"Hello, ladies, I hope your day is going well."

"Thank you," Cookie tells the reporter. "We are very excited to get Sugar home."

"So tell me a little bit about how this family reunion happened in the first place."

"Well, two Christmases ago, I gifted my sister one of those DNA genealogy thingamajigs. Honestly, I'd forgotten all about it until last Christmas. I guess my sister sent it in before she deployed, and lo and behold, voila, we found out that we had a long-lost aunt.

"Beau and I had our niece and nephew with us for the holidays. Sugar and her husband, Clint, couldn't be with the family because of job obligations. We were here at the Inn, and Clint had arranged for Sugar to FaceTime home a few days before Christmas. Stella and Stanley were so excited to see and talk to their mom—heck, we all were. Little did we know, however, that Sugar, Clint, and Beau had schemed up this elaborate surprise for me.

"My sister and our long-lost Aunt Eve had talked several times on the phone. My fiancé, Beau, had even arranged a trip to Maine so that he could meet her in person. He told me he was going to buy fresh lobsters. I didn't question him because he does make that trip a few times a year so that our Inn has fresh seafood for the holidays. To make a long story short, Beau booked her to stay at our Inn during the Christmas holiday season.

"I was out of town when Aunt Eve arrived at the Inn. I'd been in West Virginia with Stella and Stanley. When we got back to the Inn, all of the guests were already registered and settled in for their Christmas with us. Honestly, even if I had been there when she arrived, I wouldn't have known Eve from Adam—no pun intended."

This got a laugh from the audience.

"Neither Sugar nor I had ever seen any pictures of our birth mother, so I wouldn't have recognized any similarities between our mother and her twin sister, Eve. As you can probably guess, they were born on Christmas Eve.

"Anyhow, let's get back to the FaceTime call from Afghanistan. Sugar reminded me of the genealogy gift from the Christmas before. Then she gave me the news of an aunt, and that she was our mother's identical twin. I felt a huge lump in my throat. I could barely ask, 'What was her name?' Then a soft voice from the back of the room said, 'Eve.' I was clueless. Then she stepped forward, separating herself from the rest of our guests, and said, 'Aunt Eve.'

"I got an instant chill, and my arms filled with goosebumps. As I turned around, it was as if I was seeing my mother for the very first time."

Just about that time, a parade of fire trucks, ambulances, and squad cars could be seen coming down the lane. They were all blaring their sirens and flashing their lights. Yes, Sergeant First Class Sugar Smithhouse was being paraded home.

The reporter told her cameraman to keep filming the homecoming, but at the family's request, they needed a few minutes for hugs and kisses before the interview continued.

Sugar had only one foot out of the car when she was pretty much tackled by her little darlings. Stella and Stanley were so excited to have their mother home for good. To make matters even better, this was Smithhouse's final deployment. Mom and Dad Lawson were next to greet their daughter, and then little sister Cookie screamed, "Welcome home, Sis!" as she joined in on the hug-a-thon.

Beau was recording everything on his phone as it unfolded. Clint was patiently waiting for his chance to embrace his wife. She ran over to him and leaped into his arms. He swung her around like she was a rag doll, then kissed her like he'd been waiting for ten months.

Last but not least, Sugar walked over to her Aunt Eve. She took her hands into hers and said, "Please, just let me look at you for a minute." She began to cry—happy tears. Her aunt embraced her and ran her aged fingers through her niece's hair. Then she whispered into her ear, "It's lovely to finally meet you, my sweet child."

Everything felt right in the world. Then the recently retired vet waved for the reporter to come over and join them. "Good evening again, this is Barbra Lancaster reporting from the Lawson Inn outside of Faith, Vermont. We are welcoming home Sergeant First Class Sugar Smithhouse from her final deployment." The audience went crazy as sirens blared and lights flashed.

After another short interview, Sugar thanked everyone for the warm welcome home. "But now," she added, "we have a wedding to plan." The family walked into the Lawson Inn, and the reporter signed off. The parade's vehicles retreated back down the lane.

Loretta and Larry Lawson, Sugar and Cookie's adoptive parents, had prepared a wonderful welcome-home and welcome-to-the-family meal. The entire family sat down in the main room of the inn and enjoyed a wonderful afternoon together, catching up and getting to know one another.

One week later, Cookie and Beau got married at the family's church on the corner of Cherry and Maple Streets, right there in Faith, Vermont. Family and friends gathered at the inn for the wedding reception following their vows. The bride decided to keep the Lawson name out of respect for the family that gave the sisters such a safe and loving home.

CHAPTER TWO
SUITCASE SURFING AND GOODBYES

Hello, my name is Stanley Smithhouse. I am 8 years old. I have an 11-year-old sister named Stella. She has the same last name too. We live in High Point, West Virginia. My daddy is the sheriff, and my mommy is in the service. It is December 21, 2022, and for the second time in the past six years, my mommy is not home for Christmas. Daddy is at work a lot, so when mommy is away, our Aunt Cookie comes to stay with us.

Aunt Cookie is from Faith, Vermont. This is also where my mommy grew up. My grandma and grandpa ran an inn on the outskirts of town, and to this day, it is still in our family. Their names are Larry and Loretta Lawson. That is also Aunt Cookie's last name. She is now the innkeeper since my grandparents decided to retire. When Aunt Cookie comes to stay with us, her boyfriend, Beau, is in charge at the inn.

Aunt Cookie refuses to call him a boyfriend. My mommy always teases her about this. "You just need to tie the knot already!" Aunt Cookie says, "He is my Beau, not my husband." Everybody always laughs when she says that. I'm not quite sure why it is funny, but I laugh too.

We spend every Christmas in Faith with Aunt Cookie. This year, however, neither mommy nor daddy will be with us for the holiday. Daddy is very busy at work this year. He already promised one of his deputies the time off, so daddy is stuck back home. I'm not sure if he's more upset about missing Christmas or the fact that he will not be able to turkey or goose hunt. I am very proud of both mommy and daddy. Every time that we are out and about as a family, people always thank my mommy for her service. I don't completely understand what she does, but it must really be important.

My daddy is popular too. The town of High Point had a parade in his honor last Christmas. They also gave him a key to the city. I didn't know it locked up, but I guess it can if you need a key. Anyway, there was a fire in town, and my daddy saved two little girls and their puppy, Pointer. Dad claims that Pointer was the real hero because he led him to where the little girls were hiding from the flames.

My sister Stella is upstairs packing for our trip to Aunt Cookie's inn. I've been packed and ready to go for a week. Dad says that I've been wearing the same underwear because I have the rest of them in my suitcase already. I think he is joking, but what he doesn't know is that I have worn the same pair for the last two days.

I'm out on the front porch waiting for Daddy to get home. He is taking a long lunch break so that he has some time with us before we leave town. I'm watching Aunt Cookie as she tries to cram everything into the back of her car. She doesn't know it, but I can hear her cussing at her trunk. She says, "No, I'm not swearing at you!" She has her phone tucked under her ear against her shoulder as she's talking to Beau. She tells Beau that she has to hang up because she sees Clint coming down the street.

From upstairs, I can hear my loudmouth sister screaming, "Daddy is home! Daddy is home!" She comes barreling down the stairs. She hits the rug at the landing and slides clear across the hardwood floor. We both love doing this. We call it staircase surfing, but my mommy calls it dangerous. She screams at us, "One of these days, you're going to crack your noggin wide open."

Dad and Aunt Cookie come in off the porch. He says, "I had two presents for both of you to open, but I see there has been some staircase surfing going on, so maybe we'll wait till after Christmas." Stella quickly straightens out the rug and promises that she won't surf anymore. Aunt Cookie chuckles and says, "We all know that is a lie," then she winks at Stella.

Daddy told us that after lunch we could open the two presents, but the rest would have to wait until Christmas Day at the inn. We sat down and had a quick lunch. Aunt Cookie made grilled cheese and tomato soup—Daddy's favorite cold-weather meal.

Then Stella and I did the dishes in a flash. Daddy handed us a small package to open first. We each tore them open. Stella gave me a confused look, as I did her too.

"Oh, batteries. Thank you, Daddy."

He looked at Aunt Cookie, and they both laughed. "Maybe you need to open up the second present too."

So we each tore into that package even faster.

"Oh, Daddy, thank you! Nintendo Switches—just what we asked for!"

We were really surprised because Daddy didn't really like the idea of giving us games like these. He said they make kids lazy. But he also knew how long of a trip it was to Aunt Cookie's inn, so he thought they might help keep us occupied to and from Vermont. I honestly think Aunt Cookie was more grateful for the gifts than either of us kids.

Daddy made us promise, however, not to spend the whole week doing nothing but playing with those silly gadgets. We promised Daddy. We both gave him big bear hugs, and then it was time for us to be on our way. We piled into Aunt Cookie's car, and Dad made sure we were all buckled up. He leaned in through the window and gave us both goodbye kisses. Then he climbed into his squad car and escorted us out of town. As we left for the highway, he sounded off the sirens, sending us on our way.

CHAPTER THREE
CHRISTMAS MUSIC AND COUNTING LICENSE PLATES

Aunt Cookie called out, "How many hours till we reach the Poconos?"

"We will be there just in time for supper," Stella cried out.

The Poconos was the halfway point between High Point and Faith. Aunt Cookie always said that we could make it in one day if one of us "half-pints" was big enough to take the wheel for a while. But since you're both little snot-nosed kids, we'll have to make it a two-day trip. That day, we listened to Christmas music and played with our new gadgets. Stella and I were also busy counting cars with different state license plates. Whoever found the most on the trip got a head start looking for the pickle on Aunt Cookie's big Christmas tree. Her tree was always really tall; it went all the way up to the loft that overlooked the Main Room in the Inn.

She always waited for us to put the angel on top of the tree. We had to go all the way up the open staircase, then across the loft to get to the top of the tree. Then, one of us would have to lean clear over the railing to put the angel where she belonged. Every year, we took turns putting her in place. This year was Stella's turn. Beau would hold onto the back of our pants as we leaned over the railing. Aunt Cookie and

Mommy both loved that angel; they said she watched over the Inn during the Christmas holiday season.

The angel was blown out of thick glass, the kind you'd find in a stained-glass church window. Aunt Cookie and Beau always picked out a tree with a sturdy branch at the top. Every year, she reminded us to be very careful because that angel had been in the family since they were babies.

Tomorrow, Aunt Cookie will turn down the Christmas music, and we will turn off our gadgets because, on the second day of our trip, she always tells us their family Christmas story. This is the story of how Mommy, Aunt Cookie, and Loretta and Larry Lawson became one happy family.

Well, Stella was right on with her timing. We pulled into our Poconos hotel right around suppertime. It was not a fancy place, but it was well taken care of. The proprietors were longtime friends of Grandma and Grandpa Lawson. They always looked forward to our visits and saved their best room for us.

We parked the car and lugged our suitcases into the room. Stella and I always tried to argue over who got which bed. This argument never lasted long because Aunt Cookie always took the one closest to the door. She told us to go into the bathroom and get washed up before supper.

As we were in the bathroom, I could hear Aunt Cookie talking to Beau. She was filling him in on how our trip was going. At the end of their conversation, she told him that she couldn't wait to see him tomorrow and that she loved him very much.

Stella came skipping out of the bathroom, mocking Aunt Cookie, making kissy noises and saying, "I love you, Beau."

She hushed up Stella and told her to mind her own business because it was time to call our daddy.

Aunt Cookie dialed Daddy's cell phone, and luckily, he had time to talk. He probably knew exactly what time to expect our call because he had made the same trip so many times, too. Aunt Cookie hit the speaker button on her phone so we could both talk to Daddy.

"Is it snowing in the Poconos? Are you behaving? Has Aunt Cookie lost her mind yet? What are you going to have for supper?"

Daddy rattled off all these questions, and Aunt Cookie assured him that we had both been good as gold. Just as we were telling Daddy that we loved and missed him, his radio went off, and he had to run—but not before he said, "I love you both."

We were both a little teary-eyed, and Aunt Cookie picked up on this. She pulled us in and gave us both a big ol' bear hug.

"Now, how about we get some supper?"

We put on our coats and walked down to the café. We always sat at the counter; we liked how the stools spun around and around. Every trip, Aunt Cookie would tell us that we were going to be too dizzy to eat, but we never were.

Stella and I always had the same thing: a big whopping cheeseburger and a haystack of curly fries with melted cheese on top. Aunt Cookie always got an open-faced roast beef sandwich. (I don't know why they call it a sandwich; it only has one slice of bread on the bottom and mashed potatoes covered in gravy over the meat.) Anyhow, that was her go-to cold-weather meal, just like Daddy's was tomato soup and grilled cheese. Before we went back to our room, Stella and I always split a banana split covered in hot fudge and caramel. Aunt Cookie said she needed something a little richer and went with the house special: pecan pie à la mode covered in fresh maple syrup.

Aunt Cookie left the waitress a big tip and told her that we would see her again after the holiday. They exchanged, "Have a Merry Christmas and Happy New Year's." The waitress thanked us for coming in and told us to be good because Santa was watching.

When we got back to the room, I turned on the TV while Aunt Cookie was in the bathroom. I knew that she would tell me to shut it off because it was bedtime, but to my surprise, Rudolph the Red-Nosed Reindeer was just starting. It was one of Aunt Cookie's favorites, so she let us stay up until it was over.

Right after Rudolph saved Christmas, we had to brush our teeth and crawl into bed. Aunt Cookie tucked us in and told us, "Sleep tight, and don't let the bedbugs bite." This always kind of freaked me out, but I knew it was just a saying. After a kiss on our cheeks, we were out like a light.

CHAPTER FOUR
SNOW STORM, TIE DYE SHIRTS, AND BEADS

Bright and early the next morning, we packed the car and then stopped by the café for a donut and a coffee fill-up for Aunt Cookie. A truck driver asked us where we were off to, and Stella, of course, cried out, "We are on our way to Faith, Vermont!" She always expected that everybody would know exactly where that was.

"Oh, you're heading north," he said. "Well, you better get a move on; there is snow in the forecast for this afternoon."

Aunt Cookie thanked him for the weather update, then told us to hurry up and use the bathroom. "If we don't beat the snow, this two-day trip might turn into a three-day marathon."

For the first few hours that morning, we again listened to Christmas music and counted license plates.

Stella screamed out, "California! Nevada! Texas!" I think she cheats, to tell the truth, but who am I to argue? Honestly, I am only eight, and I don't even know all of the states, let alone how to spell or read them. But I do like the competition.

I always wanted to outdo my big sister, no matter if it was staircase surfing or state license plate hunting.

It was getting close to lunchtime, and we were all getting hungry. "Woodstock is only 40 miles away," Aunt Cookie told us. She always liked to stop there. She said we were too young to understand why, but someday, when we were older, she would explain. The town seemed to be very popular with people wearing beads, long hair, and tie-dyed shirts. The diner we stopped at also sold lots of souvenirs with a funny-looking leaf. This whole town seemed a little strange to me, but I did get a kick out of how weird everyone looked.

We had a quick bite to eat, and Aunt Cookie again refilled her coffee mug. When we got back out on the road, it was starting to snow a little heavier. All morning it had just been flurries, but now it was starting to stick to the road's surface. "Is it time yet?" I asked Aunt Cookie.

"Well, I guess now is as good a time as ever. If we wait any longer, I might have to give up on the storytelling to concentrate 100% on the blizzard conditions."

And with that, she turned down the radio, and we shut off our gadgets. The story was always the same, but that didn't matter. Aunt Cookie always told it in a way like we'd never heard it before.

CHAPTER FIVE
A BASKET, A QUILT, AND AN ANGEL

Christmas was less than one week away—kind of like it is right now. Your mommy and I were so very excited. We had been very good all year.

We sat down and wrote our letters to Dear Santa Claus, hoping that our Christmas wishes might be answered this year.

Your mommy and I were separated by three years, just like you two are. I sometimes wonder if your mommy didn't plan that out. On Christmas Eve, your Grandma and Grandpa Lawson arrived early to set up for the candlelight service that evening. Larry got out of their truck first and then opened the door for his wife, Loretta. She's always said that, throughout their entire marriage, he's been the perfect gentleman.

As they walked up to the front of the church, they saw a basket inside the glass entryway. Loretta called out to her husband, "Do you hear that?"

"What do you hear, my dear?" Larry replied.

She frantically ran ahead of him and threw open the glass doors. "Now can you hear them?"

"Yes, I do."

They could hear the cry of a baby.

The basket had a quilt lying over it. There was a glass Christmas angel dangling from the basket's handle. Loretta lifted up the quilt and yelled to her husband, "Larry, there are two baby girls! Who could leave their babies like this?"

She grabbed them both and carried them into the warm church. A manger scene was set up next to the pulpit because the children's choir was going to perform for the congregation that evening. Loretta sat in a pew and nestled close to the baby girls, trying to keep them warm. She covered them with the quilt and sang "O Holy Night," trying to calm them down.

The little girls had on mittens. The oldest had the name Sugar sewn on hers, and the little baby's mittens said Cookie. This is how your grandma figured out our names. That night's Christmas Candlelight Service was truly a miracle.

The men of the congregation gathered in the back of the church, listening to Larry tell their story. The ladies of the guild gathered around Loretta and the baby girls. They couldn't get over how cute those poor baby girls were. The minister's wife warmed up some milk for the hungry tots. For the remainder of the night, the ladies were cooing and awing over your mommy and me.

The mayor and sheriff of Faith County gra9nted your Grandma and Grandpa temporary guardianship until someone came forward to claim us. Two years passed, and no one ever came looking for your mommy or me. So, on Christmas Eve, in front of the Honorable Judge Steirs, we were officially adopted by Loretta and Larry Lawson.

They had tried for years to start their own family, but it was not meant to be. Your Grandma Loretta said on more than one occasion that God had a plan in mind for them, and that plan was to be our parents. Your Grandma and Grandpa Lawson were very good to your mommy and me. They provided us with love, security, stability—and love. Wait, I already mentioned love, didn't I? Well, that's how important we were to our new mommy and daddy.

Grandma Loretta kept the beautiful glass angel because she said that it had looked out for us and kept us safe until we found you both. She also kept the quilt that lay over us and kept us warm.

It was beautifully stitched and sewn with golden threads. The scenery on the patterns had a country theme. There were mountains, rivers, and evergreen trees. There were also cabins, barns, and some farm animals. Someone, or a group of ladies, took a lot of time sewing and stitching that quilt together.

Stella interrupted her Aunt Cookie to let me know that the same quilt is the one that hangs in the Main Room of her inn.

"Well, yes, it is," Aunt Cookie replied. "As long as I'm on this earth, that quilt will hang right where it is."

Again, Stella puts her two cents into the story.

"Mommy says that it will belong to me someday!"

"Well, she is right about that, Stella, but I hope you're not in too big of a hurry for it."

"No!" Stella tells her aunt that she will be patient. Aunt Cookie laughs at her niece's answer.

"I have to pee." Aunt Cookie looks at me and giggles.

"Is that all you have to say?"

"Well, I really do."

"Ok, we need to stop for gas and stretch our legs anyhow. I promise we'll hit the next gas station, Stanley. Can you hold it till then?"

"I hope so."

"So do I," Stella yells at her brother as she scoots as far away from him as she can.

"Oh look, there's one at the next exit."

Aunt Cookie halted story time long enough to gas up and stretch our legs.

CHAPTER SIX
NO SECRETS AMOUNGST SISTERS

The last two hours of our trip were very pretty. The road zigs and zags through the mountains of Vermont. But with the snow coming down the way it is, Aunt Cookie says it may take more like three hours. So while Stella and I were using the little boys' and girls' rooms, Aunt Cookie sent a text to Daddy and Beau to let them know our whereabouts. Then Aunt Cookie said she, too, needed to use the little girls' room. I asked her if she wasn't too old to use a "little girls'" room. She asked me if I liked that gas station. I asked her why. She said if I kept making comments like that, I might be left there! I know Aunt Cookie, and she wouldn't do that to me. I hope!

So, after Aunt Cookie again filled up her coffee mug—boy, she really likes coffee—we were back on the road.

"Okay, now where did I leave off?" Stella called out.

"How pretty the quilt was," I replied.

"Oh yes, that's right," Aunt Cookie responded. "Well, like I said, my mom, Loretta, held onto that quilt so that your mommy and I would have something that had belonged to our mother. Your Grandpa Larry was very handy. He built a cedar chest from a tree that he cut down right there in our timber. Your Grandma always said she loved that chest, but not as much as my little darlings. I loved it when she called your mommy and me that." She folded the quilt up with care and placed it into the cedar chest for safekeeping.

A few years passed by since the adoption, and I was getting to the age when little kids ask a lot of questions. I had heard your mommy and Loretta talk about the other mommy. They thought it best to be honest with me, so they never kept the truth about the adoption from me. Your mommy could faintly remember our mom, so they knew that sisters could not keep a secret like that from one another. We sat down as a family, and as they told my story, I was kind of sad at first. But the way Loretta told the tale made me feel very lucky to be part of their family. From that point forward, I never second-guessed how much I was truly loved by the Lawson family.

Your mommy knew where Loretta kept the quilt. From time to time, we would sneak peeks at it. Sometimes your mommy and I would go to the local sewing shop with Loretta. Sometimes the ladies would gather in the back room and put together quilts. We would sit quietly and watch them as they sewed and stitched the patterns together. The ladies worked endless hours to reach perfection. They probably didn't think we were listening that closely to them, but we also learned a lot about the town's gossip.

Some nights, when your mommy and I lay in bed, she would tell me stories that she imagined. She hoped that our mom worked on our quilt the way those ladies did; maybe even she worked on it with her mommy, too. These stories were our little secret bedtime stories, and they always made me feel warm inside, even on the coldest Vermont evenings.

CHAPTER SEVEN
SANTAS LIST AND A PRAYER

Well, another Christmas Eve was now just a few days away. Your mommy asked Loretta if maybe they could start a new tradition. She asked if it would be okay to lay the quilt at the foot of their bed during the Christmas season. Loretta thought that was a very heartfelt idea, so she agreed. That night, she opened up the cedar chest and laid the quilt over the rack on the wall so it could air out.

The following day, we placed the quilt across the foot of our bed. We took the time to carefully make sure it was perfectly even and that there were no creases. Larry said that a master sergeant in the Army could have bounced a coin off of it. Both your mommy and I were mesmerized by the artful décor of the quilt. That night, she changed up our secret story just a bit. She told me that she imagined our mommy living in one of the cabins that was so beautifully stitched into the fabric. She wondered if maybe she had milked a goat or cow outside one of the barns. These were very warm and happy thoughts that she filled my head with. But once the stories were over and we lay there in silence, I always got kind of sad, wondering why a mommy didn't want her baby girls anymore.

We both loved the Lawsons very much, but every year, your mommy would still ask Santa Claus for the same thing. In her letter to Saint Nick, she would ask him to please bring her mommy home. One year, she asked Loretta if this was being selfish because she knew she had so much more than a lot of other children. Your grandma could not believe how mature and loving your mommy was. She would hug Sugar and tell her that it is only natural for her to wonder about her mom and that it is okay to feel the way she does.

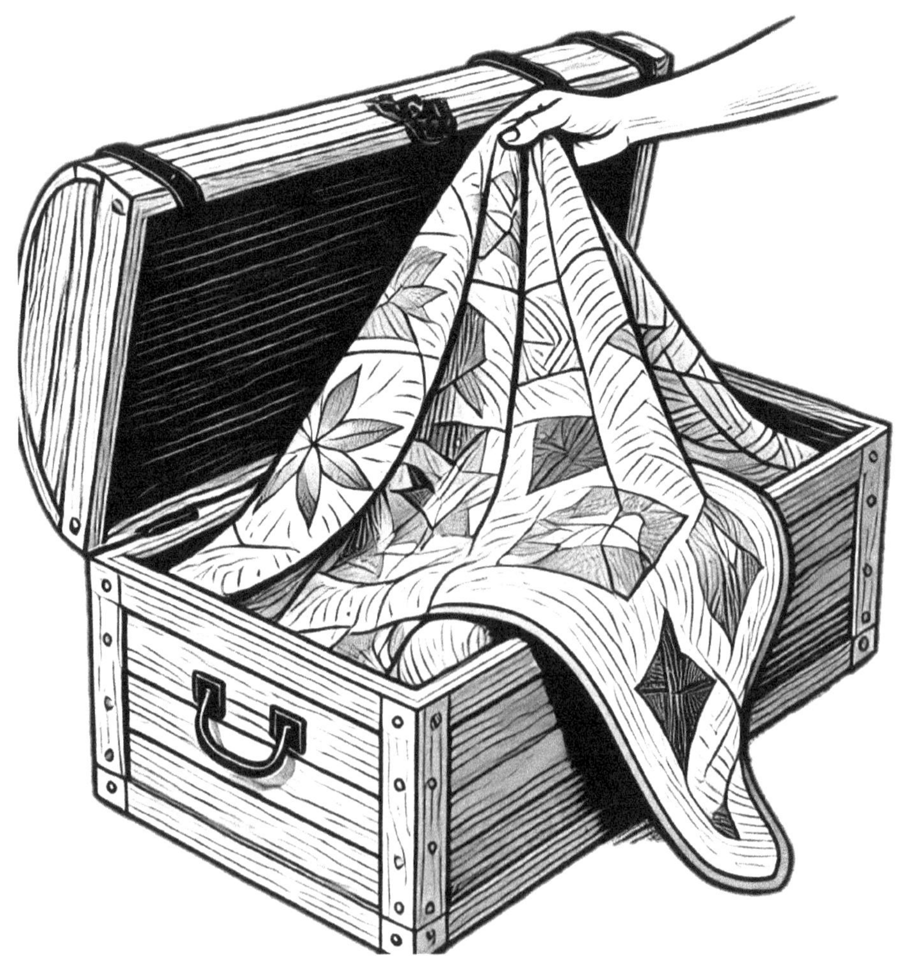

Year after year, we would get the quilt out of the cedar chest as Christmas drew near. And every year, your mommy would share with me the stories that the quilt whispered to her. I looked forward to those stories all year, and when those cold December nights arrived, your mommy always warmed us up with her beautiful imagination. Then one year, when your mommy and I were a little older, she didn't ask Santa for her mommy. Loretta noticed this and asked your mommy if everything was all right. Your mommy started to cry and told her that Santa cannot make miracles happen. Your grandma Loretta was heartbroken and told her, "Oh, darling, but he did. It was Christmas Eve when you and your sister came into our lives. If that's not a miracle, then I don't know what one is. But honestly, I think it was more Jesus answering my prayers than Santa Claus."

Your mommy's tears turned into smiles, and she gave Loretta a monster bear hug. Then she told us that we had better get up to bed; after all, it is Christmas Eve, and you know who will be coming shortly. We gave Loretta and Larry goodnight kisses and headed up to bed. After tucking us in, they stood in the doorway as we knelt at the sides of our bed and said our prayers.

Now I lay me down to sleep. I pray the Lord my soul to keep. If I should die before I wake, I pray to my Lord to take. I climbed up into bed, but your mommy continued to kneel. She said, "Jesus, I'm sorry for asking Santa Claus to bring my mommy back, because now I understand that we were your Christmas gift to Loretta and Larry."

Your Grandma Loretta grasped onto her husband's arm so tightly that he could hardly bear it. Then they watched your mommy crawl up into bed and give me a goodnight hug and kiss. Loretta and Larry quietly slipped away from the door. That night, your Grandma Loretta also said a prayer to Jesus, thanking Him for the greatest two gifts anyone could ever receive on a Christmas Eve.

CHAPTER EIGHT
A DIARY, AND A RECIPE FOR SUGAR-COOKIES

Your mommy tossed and turned all night. Was it the excitement that children experience the night before Christmas, or could it have been the unsettling feelings she had from not asking Santa for her mommy that year? She felt blessed by what your Grandma had told her, but she still felt guilty for giving up hope that we would ever know the real story of our mommy.

Christmas morning arrived, and I was up first, shaking you awake. "Get up! Wake up! Wake up, it's Christmas! Let's go find out what Santa brought us." Your Grandpa Larry was already downstairs making coffee for your Grandma. She was still upstairs making their bed when we ran into their room all excited. We grabbed her hands and led her out of the bedroom. We flew down the stairs, and Loretta followed close behind. Stella cut in on Aunt Cookie's story one more time. She asked Aunt Cookie if they staircase-surfed at the bottom.

"Well, maybe we did, but I'll never admit to it." I told my sister that meant they did, and we all laughed.

Aunt Cookie said, "Enough with the interruptions! Do you want me to finish the story or not?" "We'll be quiet, I promise," Stella spoke for us both. "Okay, then, back to Christmas morning." Your Grandma and Grandpa sat in their loveseat, watching as we ripped open our packages. It always brought them so much joy to watch their little darlings on Christmas morning. If only it didn't go by so darn fast.

We were playing with our new dolls and modeling our new outfits. Loretta went into the kitchen to take a coffee cake out of the oven.

Your Grandpa told us to take our new clothes upstairs, and while you're up there, make your bed. We wanted to stay downstairs and play with our dolls, but we knew better than to argue. Kids did what they were told back in the day. Stella and I looked at each other and rolled our eyes. We knew that Aunt Cookie was trying to make a point. "Well, did you get that jab?" Aunt Cookie asked with a silly grin on her face. "Yes, Aunt Cookie, loud and clear." "Okay, good, now let's finish this story."

A few minutes had passed since we had gone upstairs. Then Loretta and Larry heard your mommy screaming. They had never heard her sound quite like that before. They ran up the stairs to see what on earth was happening. Grandma almost knocked Grandpa over the railing. As they looked into our room, they saw your mommy curled up in the quilt. She was clutching a small leather booklet. "What do you have there, darling?" your Grandma asked.

"I was picking up the quilt because it had fallen on the floor during the night. I noticed something sticking out of a small tear in the corner. I tried to be very careful not to pull on the thread, but I wanted to see what it was. Look what I found." She handed Loretta the small leather booklet. "I think Jesus answered my prayers from last night."

Lo and behold, it was a diary that had belonged to a girl named Christmas. As we thumbed through the pages, we figured out that it must have belonged to our mother.

It was written in cursive, so Loretta had to help your mommy read it. We all went downstairs to the kitchen table and spent the morning reading the diary. Come to find out,

Christmas was also an orphan, but unlike your mommy and me, she never had a nice family to take her in. She went from one foster family to another, never finding the love or stability that we got from your Grandma and Grandpa Lawson.

CHAPTER NINE
CHRISTMAS'S STORY

The diary was a bittersweet read. As it turned out, Christmas was ill. She knew that her time was nearing the end. Her final Christmas wish was also the most difficult decision of her short life. All she hoped for was a nice family to find her daughters and give them the kind of life that she never had. She spoke of one of her favorite memories: she spent a Christmas Eve service at the church where she left her daughters. Your mommy was a newborn baby on that Christmas Eve. The ladies of the church guild had just finished putting together a quilt. The minister's wife wrapped your mommy up in that quilt and told Christmas that the quilt was the church's gift to her newborn baby girl.

They spent that cold Christmas Eve with the minister and his wife. The following day, they shared their Christmas meal with the young mother and her baby. Christmas wrote in her diary that the minister's wife made the best sugar cookies, and before they left, she wrote down the recipe for her to keep.

As your Grandma Loretta turned one of the last pages of the diary, an index card fell out and landed on your mommy's foot. She picked it up, and you guessed it... yep, it was the recipe card for the Christmas sugar cookies. Loretta looked at us and explained that their mother didn't always have it so good, but her fondest memories came from that Christmas Eve at their church.

Loretta then picked up your mommy and explained to her that the recipe was their family tree. Your mommy said that this was her best Christmas ever, at least until she had you two little brats. That afternoon, your Grandma Loretta, your mommy, and I all stirred up a batch of those Christmas sugar cookies. And they were the tastiest cookies I've ever eaten.

Later that night, your Grandma Loretta taught us girls how to sew. We stitched up the corner of the quilt. That night, we slept under our mother's quilt, and neither of us tossed or turned all night. We slept like babies because our Christmas wish had finally been answered.

Well, that is the end of our story for this year's trip. Aunt Cookie looked into the car's mirror and saw that I had a hold of my sister's hand. I quickly pulled it away and wiped a tear off my cheek. She winked at me as if to say, "It's alright, little guy." She always has a way of making me feel better with just a silly wink. And with that, we pulled down the lane that led to the Lawson Inn.

CHAPTER TEN
THE SCHEME AND A FEW SURPRISES

Aunt Cookie honked her horn, and Beau hustled right out to greet us. "Boy, I was getting worried about you the way this snow has been coming down. I'm so glad you're all home now."

Stella and I grabbed one of our small suitcases, and Beau hauled in the rest of the luggage. We kicked off our snowy boots and left them by the entrance. Beau took our stuff back to our room. When he came back, he called out, "Look what I found! I do believe it is Stella's turn this year."

Beau had the stained glass Christmas angel. He handed it to Aunt Cookie, and then we all climbed up the stairs to the loft overlooking the Main Room. Aunt Cookie handed Stella the angel but first reminded her to be very careful with it. Stella leaned over the railing as Beau securely held her by the back of her britches. That is such a funny word. Daddy and Beau always call a pair of pants 'britches.' Anyway, Stella carefully put the angel on a sturdy branch, then Beau pulled her back off of the railing.

Aunt Cookie told me that Stella got to top the tree, so it was my turn to light it up. Beau handed me the cord and asked me to please do the honors. I plugged it in and wow, the tree lit up the whole Main Room. Christmas music was playing, and the handful of guests who were there for the holidays all began to cheer. Stella grabbed Aunt Cookie's arm and pointed toward the quilt that was hanging on the wall. "Look at how the golden threads glow." Aunt Cookie rested her arm on Stella's shoulder. "Isn't it beautiful?" she whispered to her niece. This day was just about perfect, except I missed my mommy and daddy.

Just as I was about to tear up again, the phone rang. Beau said, "Well, I wonder who that might be." I looked across the room, and that's when I saw my mommy on the big screen TV. We all flew down the staircase, and guess what? Yep, all four of us staircase-surfed across the Main Room floor. That's when I could hear my mommy say, "If I've told you once, I've told you a thousand times, one of these times you're going to break open your noggin." We all laughed, and Aunt Cookie gave me one of her it's all okay winks. Mommy yelled, "I saw that, sis!" Aunt Cookie cried out, "Busted." Mommy said the tree looked beautiful, as always, and "Look, there's my quilt." She held her hands up to her chest and made a heart shape with her fingers. "Thank you, sis, you mean the world to me." Aunt Cookie made the same gesture back to her big sister.

Mommy then held up a tray of Christmas sugar cookies. "Thank you, I received your care package, and my troop loves your cookies." Then mommy said, "I got a very special present for you too, little sis." Aunt Cookie looked at her sister and told her that she didn't have to get her anything. "Well, I did, and in all honesty, you helped make it all possible." Aunt Cookie seemed a little confused. "Okay, sis, you've piqued my curiosity. What could you be talking about?" Mommy asked her sister if she remembered what she and Beau had got her last year for Christmas. Beau chimed in, "Oh, yeah, we got you one of those genealogy DNA things." "Oh, that's right, I almost forgot about that," Aunt Cookie replied.

"Well, sis, as it turns out, Christmas had a twin sister."

"Christmas? Twin sister?" At this point, Aunt Cookie was even more confused. Then, suddenly, her eyes opened wide and her jaw dropped to the floor. "Do you mean Christmas? Christmas from the diary? Christmas, our mother?"

"Yes, sis, that Christmas. She contacted me a few months back, and we talked over the phone several times. Then we schemed up this elaborate plan to surprise you during the holiday. I know Christmas Eve is still a couple of days away, but this will be my only chance to see your face, so surprise!"

"You mean she is still alive? Where does she live? Does she have a family? What is her name?" Aunt Cookie rattled off question after question, and all my mommy said was, "Merry Christmas, little sis!"

Aunt Cookie again asked what her name was. Then there was a commotion coming from the back of the Main Room. The guests seemed to be parting as an elderly lady separated herself from the rest of the guests. "Eve." Aunt Cookie turned and looked at her. "Eve, my name is Eve. My older sister by five minutes was named Christmas; she was your mother." Aunt Cookie just stood there, staring at this woman she'd never seen before. Then something happened that I'd never seen before—Aunt Cookie began to cry. Was she happy? Was she sad? Was she mad? She then wiped the tears away from her face and grabbed Bcau's hand very tightly. She looked around the room, wondering who else may have been involved in this scheme. Then Aunt Cookie looked at me, and it was my turn to give her one of those classic winks. This made her smile.

Mommy then told her sister that Beau and Clint were in on it too. Aunt Cookie punched Beau in the arm and screamed, "How in the heck did you pull this off?" Then she gave him a hug. Next, Aunt Cookie walked over to her Aunt Eve and gave her a big hug too. "How is this possible?" Well, I guess we have a lot to talk about, but all I really know about your mother is from our very early childhood. Somehow, we were separated and never found each other. Honestly, I was too young to even remember that I had a sister. Sugar has told me all about you, how you were both raised by a good family. She told me the story about the diary, the quilt, the Angel. Then she turned to Loretta and Larry Lawson and thanked them for raising some great young ladies. Finally, Great Aunt Eve turned toward me and said, "It's an honor to meet you, Stella and Stanley."

Aunt Cookie looked at Beau and asked him, "You didn't make her pay for her room, did you?" Everyone in the room laughed, and he said, "Of course not; she is family." A loud buzz came from the big screen TV. Mommy said, "Well, my darlings, my time is up. I love you, Stella. I love you, Stanley. I hope you both have a very Merry Christmas. I'll see you all at Easter time when I get home." Then the screen got fuzzy, and Mommy was gone.

Aunt Cookie shut the big TV off and turned on the Christmas music again. "Hey Beau, go down and get a couple of the bottles of our best stuff; we have some celebrating to do." Everyone was having a great time getting to know Great Aunt Eve. All of the guests thought that it was so special that the two pairs of sisters had similar holiday names—Christmas and Eve, and Sugar and Cookie.

About an hour later, Daddy called to talk to us all. "Hey, Cookie, how did you like that surprise?" She yelled at him, "How in the heck did you keep that from me all this time?" "It wasn't easy; you're the nosiest sister-in-law I have." "Clint, I'm the only sister-in-law you have!" Then Daddy said, "Well, how about one more surprise?" Aunt Cookie threw her arms up in the air and screamed, "What? This day has already been so crazy, I don't know if I can handle another surprise." Then Daddy told her to turn around.

So Aunt Cookie turned around and saw Great Aunt Eve standing between Stella and me. Behind us was Mommy's quilt. We stepped aside, and there was Beau on one knee. He said, "Cookie, would you please make me the happiest Beau in the world?" I then handed him a little box, and he took out a shiny ring. "Baby, would you please marry me?" Aunt Cookie turned and looked at my daddy and shook her finger at him. "Yeah, I know you were in on this!" Daddy laughed. Then she turned back and looked at Stella, Aunt Eve, Larry, and Loretta—they were all holding their breath. Finally, she looked at me. I winked at her, and she winked back at me. I knew her answer before she screamed it out. "Yes! Yes! Yes! Beau, I will marry you!"

Well, I hope you enjoyed our story. Mommy made it home safe the following spring, just in time for the Easter wedding. We still spend every Christmas in Faith at Aunt Cookie and Uncle Beau's Inn. That was the last Christmas that Mom had to spend away from her family. We were lucky enough to have several more Christmases with Grandma and Grandpa Lawson and Great Aunt Eve.

The End

ABOUT THE AUTHOR

David M. Gullstrand is a lifelong resident of a small town in western Illinois, where he was raised as the middle child of two sisters. Surrounded by the love and guidance of his grandparents and parents; married for over 65 years, he graduated from Western Illinois University with a major in Sociology and a minor in Journalism. He went on to dedicate 34 years as a juvenile detention counselor while raising his son as a single father. Now retired, David enjoys woodworking, doting on his grandchildren, and spending time with Great Dane, Gretchen. Writing is his latest adventure, and *The Christmas Quilt* marks his debut as an author.